Diary of an Among US Crewmate

First Time In Space

Mark Powers

Crewmate Log 1

Wow, I can't believe it's happening. After a year of training at Mira Space Academy, I have finally graduated to become a crewmate on a spaceship! Right now, I am on a transport ship that will take me to the Skeld, which will be the ship where I will live for the next six weeks. We will deliver supplies to the planet Polus and then turn around and come back.

Space explorers discovered the planet Polus about four years ago, and our federation has been putting together a plan to make it habitable for people.

Today, we had a big graduation ceremony. Fifty of us started the training a year ago, but only twenty-seven graduated. I'm the youngest person ever to graduate. Five years ago, they never would have let me train, but they need more people to help transport.

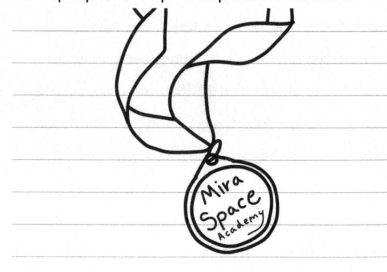

The ceremony was important. We had it in the main ceremony room at Mira Space Academy, with silver banners lining each of the walls. They even gave us a graduation medal! My family all came, including my little brother and sister. My mom cried and said she would miss me. My dad said he was proud that I would be a transport crewmate. I was too embarrassed to tell them I would miss them.

It was funny, though. One of the other recruits hid a space cat in his uniform and released it just as the professor was reading out the cadets' names. A space cat looks like a regular Mira cat, except it has leathery skin like a lizard. The space cat ran under everyone's seats and made one lady scream. I guess space cats like water because after the ceremony and fell asleep in the bowl full of punch, with only its head sticking out. Someone had to scoop it out and rinse off the red. It was so funny.

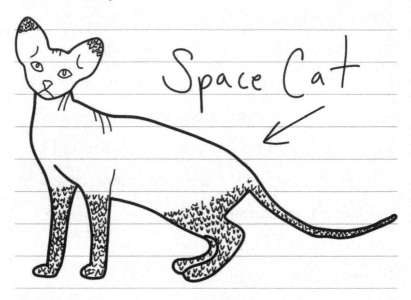

Space Cat

I will miss all the friends I made at Space Academy. The other recruits were assigned to other transports so that I won't know anyone on my ship.

As a graduation present, my mom gave me this tablet so I can record everything that happens when I'm on the spaceship. She said it's important to record what I learn and what happens while I'm on the ship. I'm excited because I can also use it to play video games in my free time.

I will sleep on this transport vessel tonight. Tomorrow morning, I will reach my new ship and meet the rest of my crew.

Each of the ten crewmates is assigned a different color uniform. That is how we will tell each other apart. Even though everyone has names, most people call each other by the color of their uniform. I will be Lime, which is good because it is one of my favorite colors. I guess the last person that was Lime on the ship was injured and had to stay at Mira HQ to recover. For some reason, no one at the academy wanted to be red. I'm not sure why.

This is my first time in space. It was weird to

watch Mira HQ and earth disappear into the black starry sky.

I would never tell anyone this, but I'm a little scared. There were all sorts of rumors at the academy about bad things happening on transport ships to Polus. No one could ever tell what bad things happened, so I think they were just trying to scare me. I'm sure they are just rumors, and nothing terrible will happen. See, I'm just freaking myself out. Nothing terrible is going to happen. This trip is going to be awesome.

Crewmate Log 2

I am officially in my bunk of the Skeld!

This morning, our ship docked on the Skeld. The door opened, and there was a second door, called the airlock, in case the first door fails.

There were all the crewmates standing in the Cafeteria, where the outer doors are.

Here are the different colors that the crewmates wear: Blue, White, Red, Cyan, Green, Purple, Brown, Yellow, Pink, and Lime, which is my color. On some ships, they have Orange and Black as well. The Captain of the ship wears green. He said he insists on running a well-organized ship, but he seems fair. Some of the other crewmates said he was on one of the vessels that discovered Polus.

The Captain asked me if I had brought any weapons aboard. I told him I didn't have any weapons. He was adamant that weapons were not allowed on board and there would be severe consequences if he found out that I had smuggled anything aboard.

Um, no, I didn't.

It's weird being on the ship because we can't

see each other very well. Our suits cover our whole body, and there is only a small window to see out. I think we can take off our masks when we eat, but otherwise, we have to wear our spacesuits at all times. That way, if there is a perimeter breach in the ship, we will still be safe.

Me in my SPACE SUIT!

All the other crewmates seemed nice. Brown came and talked to me after I met everyone.

She was nice. I'm glad I have one friend here. There are a few young crewmates like me, and brown is one of them.

Red wasn't very friendly. He kept his mask down the whole time, so I never got to see his face. Everyone else said hello and introduced themselves, but Red didn't. He just hung back and kicked the ground with his foot.

The Skeld is much bigger than I thought it would be; even though I'd seen the map of what it looked like on the inside, I imagined it smaller than it is.

Since I'm the newest crewmate, I get to help out all over the ship. All the other crewmates are going to teach me how to maintain their part of the Skeld. I will move from section to section until I know how to do all the ship tasks. I'm most excited about a job where I will shoot the asteroids, so they don't hit the ship and damage it.

The Captain gave me some time to settle in, so I'm in my bunk. It is a small private room above the Cafeteria. Most of the crewmates have a bunk above the Cafeteria. It's the reason the Cafeteria is one of the largest areas on the ship. In addition to eating there, it is the place we hang out in our time off.

A machine in the Cafeteria can make any food you want, instantly! I asked for three different types of donuts (chocolate, maple, and a pink one with sprinkles), and it gave them all to me.

Goodnight!

The perfect donut.

Crewmate Log 3

Today was awesome and interesting. I had four donuts for breakfast, something my mom would never have let me do in a million light-years.

I got to shadow my first crewmate. When you shadow a crewmate, it means you follow them around (like a shadow), and they show you all the tasks they have to keep the ship flying smoothly through space. For the whole day, I followed White, and he showed me how the electrical works throughout the ship. I will shadow White for three days before I will move on to a different crewmate.

There is a room where all the electrical wires in the whole ship connect called Electrical. Wires connect to electrical panels all over the ship.

All the crazy electrical wires.

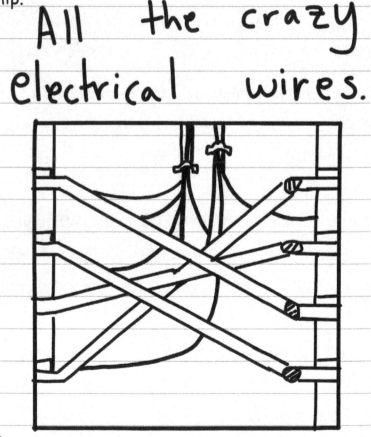

When I was at Mira Space Academy, I didn't care about Electrical, but now I think it's so cool. Without electricity, the entire ship wouldn't be able to function. It controls the lights, oxygen levels, doors--everything.

White seemed cool. He had to reprogram a panel, and he even let me connect the wires back together when he finished.

White said that sometimes wires could come undone, and it makes things malfunction on the ship. Tomorrow he will show me how to fix them when they go wrong.

Weird! The lights just flickered in a spooky way! I better go see what is going on.

Crewmate Log 3.5

That was crazy!

The lights went out all over the entire ship! Good thing I brought a little flashlight from my bunk because I couldn't see a thing. I found White in Electrical, but he said the problem wasn't there. Instead, it was a problem with some wires in Navigation. I ran there so I could help put the wires back together.

It was super strange. As we were entering Navigation, I saw Red peak around a corner. He didn't have a flashlight, and he acted like he didn't want anyone to see him. It seemed sus.

I held the flashlight as White put the wires back together. He gave the wires a strange look and said that this wasn't usually how the wires came undone. Usually, they shake loose because of space turbulence, but these looked like they had been sliced with a tool. It made me think of Red. Did he have something to do with the wires?

After White fixed the wires, we were able to get all the lights turned back on.

The Skeld was spooky when all the lights were out. It gives me goosebumps just thinking about it. When I shone my flashlight around, all the reflective metal made it look like shadows were moving everywhere.

It was fun to help White put the wires back together, but I hope that doesn't happen again.

I'm going to keep an eye on Red. I don't trust him.

After White and I re-wired the panel, Captain Green said he was glad we quickly fixed the issue. I was surprised he wasn't there sooner, though. Maybe stuff like this happens all the time, and it isn't a big deal.

Tonight, we all ate dinner in the Cafeteria. I sat by Brown.

I asked her about the lights. She said that happens sometimes, and it isn't a huge deal. It happened once during her first flight and then again a year later. She has been on fifteen trips to and from Polus.

After dinner, Brown showed me something that I've NEVER seen before. She called it a board game. I guess her Grandma gave it to her, and she used to play with it when she was a kid. I think they used to play them on Mira forever ago before all the games were on tablets. It is a game that isn't on a screen, but you put it on the table in front of you on an actual board. It was called Funopoly. My game piece was a little silver shoe. We rolled a dice and went around a board and bought properties. It was super fun! I played with Brown, Blue, and Cyan. I lost, but it was still fun.

Brown told me that next, she would introduce me to something called a card game.

This is a board game.

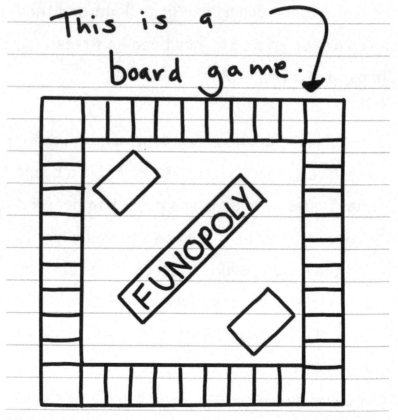

Crewmate Log Four

The last few days, I have been so busy I haven't been able to add to my Crewmate Log. I have learned all about electrical. White even let me reprogram a panel all by myself.

I've been hanging out a lot with Brown, Blue, and Cyan. Brown works in the Medbay and takes care of anyone that gets hurt. Blue works in Security. She can watch where everyone is on the whole ship to ensure everyone is safe and there are no accidents. Cyan works in Communications. I can't wait to learn how to do everything.

While I was working on the electrical, Red came into the room. I said hi. He just nodded and walked out. What's with that guy?

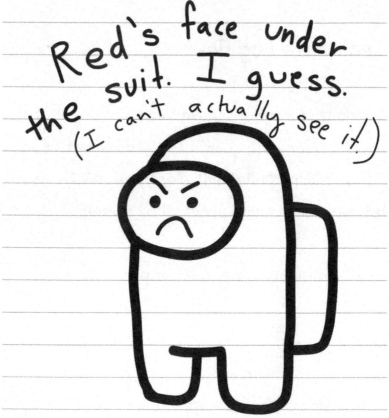

Red's face under the suit. I guess. (I can't actually see it.)

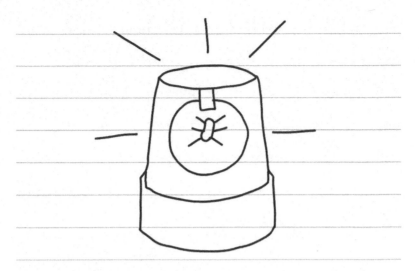

Crewmate Log Five

I jerked awake. An alarm screamed out,
"Oxygen malfunction. Oxygen Malfunction,"
over and over. A red light flashed in my room.
I stumbled out of my bunk and ran toward the
panel my communication device said I needed
to fix.

Everyone else was scrambling to fix it as well.
I was terrified. Seriously, so scared. I'd
wondered why we had to wear our spacesuit

even when we were in bed, but now I know why. Somehow a panel opened up, and the oxygen was sucked out of the spaceship. I was the second person to arrive at the malfunction. Yellow was already there, trying to close the panel. I got on the other side, and we were able to push the panel closed.

We had to rush to seal the panel after we closed it. We then had to type in a code some the ship will fill up again with oxygen. Our suits only have a little bit of oxygen stored in them. If we don't fix the problem, we will run out of oxygen before the ship can fill up with clean air.

Everyone was there trying to seal up and reprogram the ship, everyone except Red. What is that guy's problem? We could have died, and he did nothing to help.

The other crewmates talked about how strange it was that we had only been in space for four days, and we had already had a light malfunction and a perimeter oxygen breach. Then our Captain came in and heard what we were saying. He said that strange things happen in space sometimes, and it's expected. But a lot of the other crewmates have been running missions in space for years, and they said it was only on this and the last trip that things like this were happening, like the previous Lime getting injured and having to stay at Mira HQ.

I'm back in my bunk, but I can't sleep. What if bad things keep happening?

Crewmate Log 6

It has been a few days, and nothing strange has happened. It must have been just a coincidence that two bad things happened during the first week here.

Today, I got to blast asteroids! It was so cool! So far, I have learned how to do tasks in Electrical and align the engine output. Today, I was supposed to move Medbay to help Brown, but the Skeld came across an asteroid field that needed to be blasted out of the way so we could fly safely through the area. Asteroid fields don't happen super often, so instead of going to Medbay with Brown, I got to blast asteroids with Pink. Pink is a couple of years older than me, and shooting asteroids has been one of his main jobs since he graduated from Mira Space Academy. He was cool.

The Asteroids

We spent an hour shooting our way through the asteroid field. I hit a massive one.

But instead of the piece flying backward back into space, a huge chunk flew back at us.

I wanted to run away!

But when you are on a spaceship, there is nowhere else to go. I clicked the button on the asteroid laser, and I managed to shoot it right before it would have crashed into my window! Pink shot at the spot right after I did, so he would have saved us if I wouldn't have.
I hope.

Pink said I was pretty good, and if I wanted to become a full-time asteroid blaster on another ship, he could help me train.

After dinner, Brown and I played card games. We sat at a table, and she had what she called a deck of cards! We played all sorts of games with the same cards. They had all the numbers to ten, either in black or red, with some funny little symbols on them as well. It also had what she called a jack, queen, and king. You know, like the rulers that ruled Mira thousands of years ago.

It was totally fun.

I asked Brown if the Captain ever comes to hand out during the evenings. She said he had on previous trips, but hadn't in a while. That's too bad. I would like to hear his stories.

Crewmate Log 7

I can't believe what happened. I don't want to be here anymore. I want to go back to Mira HQ.

Maybe I should start at the beginning.
I was working in Medbay. Brown went to get supplies from storage. While she was gone, the alarm blared again!

For the third time since I got here.

This time it was a reactor meltdown. This one is even worse than the oxygen level because it could blow up the entire ship!

I rushed from Medbay to the reactor. I was looking at my communicator to see what I needed to do, and I tripped on something. It was a crewmate! It took me a minute to realize it was Purple. Around her spacesuit was a puddle of red, sticky blood.

I jerked back because I was so scared. And I had to help fix the reactor core before we all were blown to space dust. I called Brown on the communications device. "Lime to Brown, Lime to Brown. We have a crewmate down. I just found Purple in Upper Engine, and she's injured. I have to continue to the reactor core."

"Roger, Lime," Brown said.

I didn't want to tell Brown that I didn't know if Purple was alive or not. There was so much blood. I didn't know how anyone could survive it.

But I had to stop the reactor core meltdown, or we'd all be dead.

When I got the reactor core, I was surprised
36

to see Red and Blue were already working on the problem. I jumped in to help. We found that the wires that help power the cooling system had been cut or disabled by something. I connected the wires back together while Red and Blue restarted the system so it would work properly again.

Even though I was working, I couldn't help but think about Purple lying in the next room over. What happened to her?

When we finished, I rushed back to Upper Engine in case Brown needed any help. Purple and Brown were gone.

I went to Medbay. There Brown and Pink were hooking Purple up to all sorts of machines as she laid on the bed.

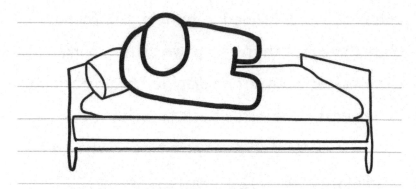

"Is she?" I couldn't help but ask.

"She's alive, barely," Brown said, not looking away from where she was helping Purple. "It looks like she was stabbed with something sharp. Whatever it was went through her spacesuit and almost killed her. If you hadn't found her, she would have been dead in five minutes."

Dead. In all my dreams about being a crewmate on a ship, I never realized that you could die on a ship. I mean, you can die anywhere, but it just seems crazy that people can die, on a ship, in space. I would never see my family or my space dog again!

What am I doing here?

"Come on, Lime," Brown said. "I need your help."

I helped Brown use all the machines in Medbay to help Purple. I'm back in my bunk, but I wanted to write down all the details.
Brown said that Purple was stabbed by something sharp, but when I was there with Purple, there was nothing around that could have hurt her. Nothing.

It makes me wonder if someone, one of the other crewmates, attacked Purple.
No, that's crazy. No one would attack anyone else. I just need to go to sleep before I think

of any other crazy ideas. I'm sure the Captain

will tell us what is going on tomorrow.

I drew my space dog, Raulph, so I can feel better.

Crewmate Log 8

The Captain gathered us together for a
morning meeting to talk about Purple. He said
there was a terrible accident and that Purple
was hurt, but that was all he said.
Brown looked over at me while he was talking. I
wonder if she thinks it wasn't an accident like I
do.

I ate my usual breakfast, four different kinds
of donuts before I headed back to Medbay.

I took my time because I didn't want to see Purple, but I had to go there eventually.

I was barely through the door when Brown grabbed me and shoved me onto this platform. She smashed a button on the side of the room, and this green light appeared. I couldn't move, and the light scanned over my whole body. The entire time, she studied a screen off to the side.

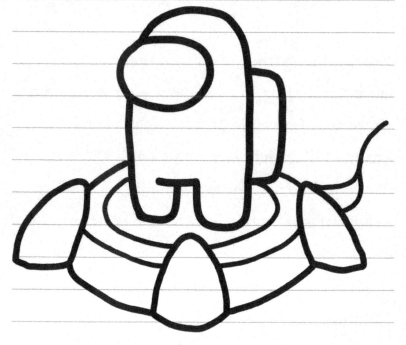

When it finished, I could move again. "What was that about?" I yelled at her.

She flipped the screen over so I could see it. "You are normal."

"Of course, I'm normal. What did you expect?"

"I just had to be sure." Brown looked over at where Purple lay unconscious on the bed. "Come on. I have to talk to you."

Brown dragged me out of Medbay and into the supply room and then again into a supply closet. The room was full of old space vacuums that, when you empty them, automatically eject the dust into outer space.

"What is going on?" I asked.

"Shhhhh," Brown said. "I had to make sure no one can hear us."

"Is this about Purple?" I said.

Brown nodded. "I don't don't think what happened to Purple was an accident."

"What do you mean?" I asked.

"When I got to Purple? There was nothing sharp around that could have hurt her. It couldn't have been an accident unless you moved something?"

"No, of course, I didn't."

"You were the first one to comm me about an injury," Brown said. "If anyone else saw it, they didn't report it."

44

"Why wouldn't they report it?"

"I don't know," Brown said. She looked around once more as if someone could be listening in our conversation. "Too many weird things have happened. I talked to a friend of mine who is a medic on another ship. Weird things started happening there, too. The crewmate found out that it was some crazy shape-shifting alien that sabotaged their ship. It even killed someone. They ended up ejecting the creature out of the ship."

I burst out laughing.

"No. There is no such thing as shape-shifting aliens."

Brown smacked me on the arm. "That's what

I said, but now I'm not sure. There have just been way too many crazy things going on. And now Purple? Her condition is stable, but she hasn't woken up yet, so I can't ask her what happened."

"So what was with the whole scan thing?" I asked.

"My friend said they eventually caught the alien because when they scanned it in the med scan, it came back as not human," Brown said.

I frowned. "Not human? Scary. I've never heard of anything like this back at Mira Space Academy."

"I think it's brand new. Nothing like this has ever happened before," Brown said. "I only heard about it through my friend. The good news is, I now know you're human. We just have to figure out who the alien might be."

SABOTAGE

"But why would Aliens come onto a ship and pretend to be a crewmate?" I asked.

"How should I know? I'm not an alien."

"I don't know that for sure," I said.

"But I'm not!" Brown said.

"Fair is fair. I want to see your scan, so I can know for sure that you're not an Alien, either."

"Fine, I'll do a scan. We need to figure out who else might be an Alien, too," Brown said

"What about Red?" I asked.

"What about him?"

I shrugged. "Don't you think he's suspicious? He didn't come to help on either of the first emergencies. But then yesterday, he was one of the first people on the scene of the reactor core meltdown."

"So?"

"So, he could have stabbed Purple and then sabotaged the reactor core, only to turn around to try and fix it."

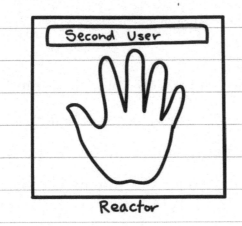

Reactor

"That's true. Red could have done that," Brown said.

"And he just isn't very nice," I said.

"Just because someone isn't nice doesn't mean they would stab you," Brown said. "But I see what you mean. Just keep your eyes open for anything suspicious."

"I will, but only after I scan you to make sure you're human."

"That's fair," Brown said.

We headed back to Medbay. Brown stood on the scanner. It said she was normal, so I'm pretty sure she's not an Alien. And if she was an Alien, why would she tell me about the aliens?

"Maybe we should stay together as much as possible, in case the Alien wants to stab us."

"Good idea. what do we do now?"

We have to figure out who the imposter is before anyone gets killed."

"But how do we do that? It could be anyone."

"I don't know. We will just have to keep an eye out for anyone who might be sus."
Brown and I stuck together for the rest of the day, and we plan to keep doing that to stay safe. It's easy because we both work in Medbay right now, but I don't know what will happen when we don't.

I'm keeping an eye out for anything suspicious, but I'm mostly going to watch out for Red.

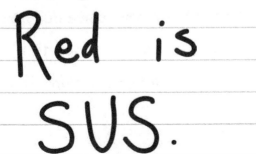

Red is SUS.

Crewmate Log 9

Today was totally crazy! In a good way.
Brown and I stayed together again all day to
make sure we were safe. We even tried to
follow Red, but we couldn't find him, which is
suspicious.

Tensions have been high since Purple was
hurt. No one has said that they think she was
attacked, but I can tell everyone thinks she
was.

But tonight, we were sitting down to dinner. Yellow tripped on a table leg, and his food tray went flying and hit Cyan on the head. Cyan got so mad that he threw his whole plate of spaghetti at Yellow. Of course, it didn't just hit Yellow, but also hit Brown, Red, and me. We had taken our helmets off to eat, but we shoved them on when the food started flying! The next thing I knew, food was flying everywhere, all over the Cafeteria! Blue ran into the room and slipped and fell on some jello someone had just thrown. There were cheeseburgers, tater tots, chocolate cake, chili, baked potatoes--everything!

Good thing we were all wearing our space suits because it would have been super gross to be covered in all that food. Everyone was laughing and having fun.

I watched Red to make sure he didn't do anything suspicious. He laughed and threw food just like everyone else. He was probably trying to blend in and act human.

The best part was when we finished, the cleaning robots came and cleaned everything up. They unhooked these long hoses from the wall and power washed the floor. The stream of water was so strong it blasted the heavy tables out of the way. At home, my mom would have made us clean. The Captain didn't even know it happened because he never eats with us. He must eat in his cabin. Come to think of it, I've never seen his face. I wonder what he looks like. He has to be old if he helped discover Polus.

Crewmate Log 10

There's been another attack.

I can't believe it. It's been a week since my last log. It was long enough that I'd thought maybe it was a fluke, and there wasn't an Imposter roaming the ship waiting for one of us to be alone so they could attack us. I think everyone was feeling better, safer.

I switched over to servicing the lower and upper engines with Red as my task.

I'll admit, I was scared.

At one point, he came up behind me. I turned around, ready to scream because he had a huge weapon in his hand.

But it wasn't a weapon. It was a tool to fix the side panel to the engine.

Phew!

He is only a year older than me and has been working on the Skeld since he graduated from Mira Space Academy.

He walked me through how to service the engines when there is a problem. I was

surprised because he wasn't mean or anything.
He showed me how to scan the machines,
and he didn't get mad when I messed up, and
he had to spend like an hour fixing what I'd
broken. I was beginning to think he was an okay
guy.

But then I heard a scream! I glanced over.
Red's back was to me, walking toward Upper
Engine. It came from Security, and I ran
towards it.

I found Blue, lying on the floor, in a puddle of blood, just like Purple.

It was so much scarier this time.

But no one else was in the room. I had been in the hall and didn't see anyone leave.

My hands shook as I hit the panic button on my com device to alert everyone that I found another body. I waited for other crewmates to come, and I noticed that the vent on the floor had scratches around it, like someone had pulled it up. Did they escape through the vents?

Brown arrived and said that Blue wasn't dead. Just like the last time, she'd been stabbed but not killed. She packed Blue onto and med transport and took her off to Medbay.

59

But then it was crazy! The other crewmates crowded around.

They all said I did it.

They said that I had found both bodies, and that was suspicious.

"It wasn't me! I was in the hall, and I heard a scream, and I ran in," I yelled.

"This happened last time," Yellow said. "You just happened to stumble on both attacked crewmates? That seems awfully sus."

"I agree," Cyan said. "He was near the attack each time."

"No, it wasn't me! I wouldn't attack anyone."

"Maybe we should eject him," Cyan said.

"That's crazy! I didn't do anything." I looked around, frantically trying to find someone who would help me.

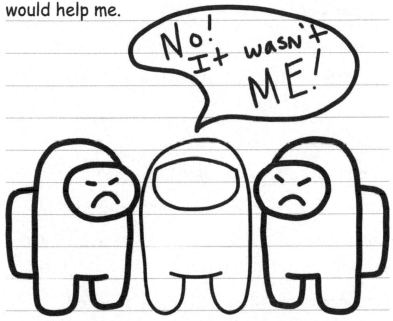

"We would be crazy to let you keep terrorizing this ship!" Yellow said.

Yellow and Cyan stepped forward and took each of my arms. They started to drag me toward the exit doors.

"No!" I screamed. "It wasn't me! Brown! Brown knows it wasn't me."

"Brown's not here," Yellow said.
Where was the Captain? They wouldn't eject me without the Captain's permission, would they?

Red stepped forward, and I thought I was a goner for sure. He was the imposter, and he would use me to draw suspicion away from him.

"It wasn't him," Red said. I was shocked.

"I was coming out of Upper Engine, headed into the hall when I saw Lime in the hall. I heard a scream and saw Lime sprint toward the sound. Why would he go towards the sound if it was him? He would want to be as far away from the body as he could be when it was found."

"Let him go," Pink said. "We have a witness that says it wasn't him."

I had to jerk my arms out of Yellow and Cyan's arms. They didn't want to let me go.

After I pulled out of their arms, I just stared at Red and didn't know what to do.

"Come on, Lime," Red said. "Let's get back to work."

I wasn't going to argue! I followed him back to the lower engine.

I was so grateful.

"Why did you save me, Red?" I asked.

"Because you didn't do it," Red said.

"How do you know?" I asked.

"I just know. And ejecting the wrong person is murder."

"That was crazy! One minute I was working on the engines, and the next, they were planning on ejecting me! If I had thought that was possible, I never would have come on this stupid ship."

"I don't blame you," Red said.

I was so embarrassed, and I said without thinking, "You know, I thought it was you."

Red stepped back in shock. "Why would you think it was me?"

I shrugged. "I don't know. You just never seemed very friendly, and during those times the alarms went off, you were never there to help. It just seemed suspicious."

"I didn't mean to seem unfriendly. I just am shy around people I don't know."

Oh. That made me feel really bad. This whole time I thought Red was a jerk, but it turns out he is just shy.

Red nodded and looked around as if he didn't want to be overheard. "I was trying to find anyone suspicious. Our other crewmate, Lime, was hurt right before we made it back to Mira HQ. And we had a few things go wrong with the ship as well, that seemed out of the ordinary."

I told him what Brown had said about her friend finding an alien imposter on their ship.

"You and Brown think we have an alien imposter aboard the ship?"

"Yep."

I told him how Brown scanned her and me, which was a way to show we weren't aliens. Red marched right to Medbay, past Brown as she was helping Blue, got on the scanner, and hit the button.

The screen flashed that everything was normal. Brown finished hooking Blue up to the machines, and then she walked over to us.

"We need to find the imposter, now, before someone dies," Brown said.

"Blue worked in security," I said, "So I bet she saw something on the security cameras, so whoever the imposter tried to take her out. "That makes sense," Brown said.

We came up with a plan on how to find the imposter before someone gets hurt again.

Crewmate Log 11

Right now, I'm writing this from Upper Engine.e

Today, most people walked around the ship in groups of two or three. No one wanted to end up the next person stabbed. It made getting tasks done more difficult, but everyone thinks it's safer. We only have a couple more days until we will arrive in Polus, so if the alien has something he wants to do, it has to be soon.

Now for our plan.

We are using me as bait.

The first attack happened in Upper Engine, and I'm hanging out here by myself. But really, my friends are hiding just outside the room, so if someone comes in, my friends can step in and theoretically-

    1. Stop the person

    2. Know who the person was

It seems like a solid enough plan to me.

None of us is going to be alone with another crewmate on the ship.

We weren't allowed to bring anything resembling a weapon on the Skeld, but I have a heavy wrench handy, just in case I need to defend myself.

Me, hanging out in
Upper Engine, realizing
this was a terrible idea.

We got all of our tasks done together and
then headed to Upper Engine. I did some
maintenance work while Brown and Red stayed
close enough for me to hear them but not see
them.

I almost feel like I can't breathe in my suit, even though I have plenty of oxygen.

But I've been hanging out here almost the entire day, and nothing has happened. Maybe the imposter doesn't try to kill people just because they hang out in a room by themselves.

I think I'm going to give up. Maybe we could try again tomorrow.

What the! The doors all just slammed shut, and the lights went out!

Log 11.5- Later that day

I didn't know what to do! I was alone in the dark.

But then I heard a sound in the room with me. A scraping, metallic sound.

I backed away until I hit the wall. I clutched the wrench to my chest.

The vent!

The sound was coming from the vent! I pounded on the door that was sealed shut. Why hadn't I brought a flashlight?

Heeeeeeellllllllpppppp! I screamed.

Behind the doors, Brown and Red yelled back, but it was too muffled. I couldn't understand what they were saying!

It was just me and whatever had crawled up through the vent.

"You," a creepy, raspy voice said. "I know you have been trying to find me. Why was it you who found the bodies both times? If it wasn't for you, I could have replaced those crewmates with my own kind, and no one would have known. You have ruined all my plans."

I was terrified, but I didn't want the creature to know that. "Show yourself!" I screamed.
The creature laughed. And laughed.

"You think you can beat me? A human has never beat me!"

The creature's footsteps as it walked toward me seemed to echo metallically.

I hung onto the tool in my hand.

I had to time it just right. I would only have one shot at using this tool as a weapon.

If only the door would open, I could escape!

I lifted my wrench, and the sound was so close, it seemed to be touching me.

I slammed the wrench down and hit something. Something squishy. It didn't feel like bones should feel.
"Ah!" The creature stumbled backward.
Just then, the door opened, and I ran out into the hall. It was still dark, but a couple of little lights lined the aisle.

My friends were there waiting for me.

"Run!" I screamed

We ran out the door, but the sound of the creature was close behind us. We passed Medbay and ran towards the Cafeteria. The lights flickered back on. Someone must have turned on the switches.

Running behind us was Green, our Captain. But it wasn't our Captain. He wasn't even human.

His spacesuit was falling off, and instead of a body, he had a gigantic mouth. It seemed to split him in half. In the mouth was a long, pointy tongue that flapped as he ran.
We ran to the Cafeteria, where White, Pink, and Cyan were waiting.

They saw us run in, and White said, "Where's the fire?"

"Not a fire!" Red said. "An Alien! Run!"

We kept running to the far wall of the Cafeteria.

White, Pink, and Cyan ran across the room with us.

Green entered the room. His tongue still lulled to one side.

"The Captain?" White said. "But how?"

The alien laughed. "I killed your Captain when you last went to Polus. I have taken his place since then."

"It was you who hurt Lime," Red said. "She was my friend."

"I know. Too bad you had to come in and save her. I could have replaced her and the others with my kind, and none of you would have ever known. Well, I will just have to kill you all and replace you anyway."

"What do we do?" Brown asked as the alien walked toward us.

We were dead. We were so dead.

"Wait, what did your friend say they did with the alien on their ship?" I whispered so the alien couldn't hear us.

"They ejected it into space," Brown said.

"That's what we have to do," I said.

"How?" Cyan said.

The alien continued to move forward. In each hand was a vicious-looking knife. His tongue looked just as sharp and deadly as the knives.

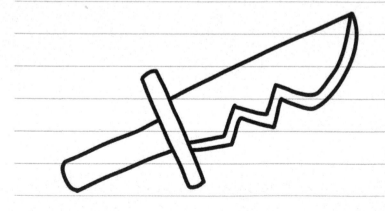

"We put him in the airlock and then open the outer door," I said.

"What??? How would we do that?" Brown asked. "The airlock won't open in space."

The alien stopped, probably trying to figure out how to attack all of us at once.

"White," I said, "can you reprogram the doors so that if we put the Alien in the airlock, we can open the outer doors, and he will get sucked into space?"

"I can try," White said. "I will have to program them so as soon as the internal door closes with the alien in there, the outer door will open, and he will be gone.

"Do it, White," I said. "The rest of us? Let's try and get him close to the airlock door. Maybe if we all grab him at once, we can do it."

We all shuffled to one side, toward the electrical panel. White opened the panel, and we crowded around him so the alien wouldn't know what we were planning.

The alien slinked toward us once more, like he was a space cat, and we were a bunch of space mice.

"How's it going back there?" I asked. The wires sparked.

"Give me a minute," White said.

"When White gives the signal, we all attack," I whispered.

The alien knocked his two knives together. It was the sound of death, and I didn't want to die. I didn't want this alien to be the last thing that I saw.

"Now!" White yelled.

We all lunged forward. The alien's tongue lashed forward and stabbed Pink in the arm. He crumpled in pain.

Cyan attacked next, and the alien's sword sliced through the air and stabbed him.

Brown, Red, and I kept running forward. We each grabbed one of the alien's arms.

He pushed us off easily.

He was stronger than all of us put together.

"Got it!" yelled White.

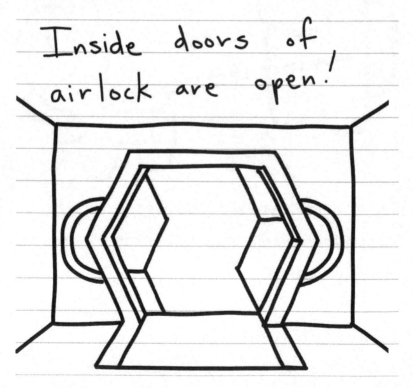

Inside doors of airlock are open!

The inner door of the airlock opened.

We had to get the alien out the doors! But we couldn't get close to him. His knives and sharp tongue prevented us from coming within five feet of him.

How could we push him out the door without getting close to him?

Then I remembered. Of course!

The hoses that the robots used to clean the floor! I ran over to the wall and unwound the hose.

"Red! Get the hose!" I yelled.

He ran over and did the same. I hit the big red button, and the water shot out, almost making me fall.

But I held on and turned the hose on the alien.
It hit him square in the back, or I guess it was
the back of the head since his mouth took up
his entire torso. He turned around, and I shot
the water into his enormous mouth. He gagged
and spit.

Red turned on his hose, and the alien fell
backward. We hit him from two sides! As he lay

on his back, the water pressure pushed him out the door. Both Red and I moved forward, Yes! It was working. He wouldn't be able to kill any of us if he was floating in outer space! He slid into the airlock.

"Close the door, White!" I screamed as I continued to keep the alien down with the stream of water.

"Now!" White said.

The doors began to close.

"Yes!" Someone yelled. "We did it!"

I kept the steady stream of water pointed at him. I wasn't going to let up until those doors closed.

But then something touched my leg. I looked down just in time to see the alien's tongue wrap around my ankles. It jerked me off my feet and pulled me out into the airlock, just as the doors closed behind me.

The door sealed me off from the rest of the ship with only the alien.

The doors! White said he would program the outer door to open as soon as the inner door was closed.

Brown screamed on the other side of the glass door. "No! Lime's out there! We have to get him."

White frantically typed into the panel.

Behind me, the alien's horrible breathing was

the only other sound.

"At least I can still kill you," the alien said.
But the sound of the opening of the outer door
cut off anything else he might want to say. The
air in the airlock rushed out, sucking the alien
and me out into the void of space.

Me in the void
of outer SPACE.

I started counting right away. I couldn't help it, even though it was a terrible idea. I only had two minutes of oxygen stored in my suit, and then I would die.

Which really sucked.

The alien had been sucked out into space as well. But he wasn't wearing his spacesuit, so he didn't last even two minutes. I had to be happy that no one would get killed on the ship, but I didn't want to die here, floating in space with an alien who'd tried to kill me and my crewmates.

I tried to swim toward the ship, but it was no matter how I struggled, I hardly moved.

"One hundred one, one hundred two," I counted. I was going to die, and the last person I saw would be an alien murderer. But then doors on the ship opened once more. Red, with a jetpack on his back, flew towards me. A thin metal cord sailed out behind him, attached to something in the airlock.

He grabbed a hold of my arm and said, "Hold on tight!"

He didn't have to tell me twice! I held on to his hand as he pushed a button, and the cord retracted back into the airlock.

"One hundred forty-five. One hundred forty-six."

It had been too long.
Everything went black.

I woke up in Medbay. Brown and Red were in the room.

"Hey!" Brown said. "You're awake!"

"I thought I was going to die," I said.

"Glad you didn't," Red said.

"How do you feel?" Brown asked.

"Tired. But i don't want to sleep anymore right now," I said. "What happened to Cyan and Pink after they got stabbed?"

"Don't worry, Cyan and Pink are just fine."

Brown brought me my tablet so I could write everything down before I miss any details.

Now that I wrote everything, I think I will go back to sleep. I'm so tired...

Crewmate Log 12

I woke up feeling much better. Brown said I'd been asleep for two days!

Nothing crazy had happened since the alien had been ejected, and so that's good.

I took a shower and put on a new Lime suit. The other one still had green sticky stuff from the alien tongue on it.

Brown also said I should get up and walk around because it would make me feel better. Dinner was about to begin in the Cafeteria, so I headed there.

When I walked in, all the other crewmates jumped out from behind the tables and yelled, "Surprise!"

I almost fell backward. I was so surprised. In Red's hands, there were a bunch of donuts stacked up to look like a cake.

"We just wanted to say thanks for saving all of us," Red said.

"And apologize for almost ejecting you," Cyan said.

"Thanks, guys," I said. "And thank you, Red, for saving me."

"Any time," Red said. "I have another surprise."

"What is it?" Brown asked.

"Lime asked me why I was never hanging out with everyone. I was trying to figure out who the imposter is, yes, but I was also doing something else."

Red went over and picked up a box and dumped it onto the table. Twenty different hats rolled over the surface.

"Hats!" Yellow said.

"Those are so cool," Pink said.

I nodded at Red. "They are cool."

Everyone reached into the pile and put one on. Brown grabbed a party hat and put it on my head.

"I'm glad we're not dead," she said.

"So am I," I said.

97

We all had a piece of the donut cake and spent the rest of the evening playing games and watching funny videos from earth. We were happy to be alive and still on our way to Polus.

I just hope nothing like this ever happens again.

The End

Check these other book from Mark Powers!

Among Us Activity Book
Includes over 50 pages of activities!

Among US
50 Tips and Tricks to Become a Master Imposter and Stellar Crewmate

Among US Blank Comic Book
100 pages, 17 layouts